To Deryk, a gift from God
—L.S.

For the child within us or beside us who is never
too old to say I love you
—M.L.

For Laura Schlessinger, for giving me this opportunity and for daring to say the things that need to be said
—D.M.

Why Do You Love Me?
Text copyright © 1999 by Dr. Laura Schlessinger
Illustrations copyright © 1999 by Daniel McFeeley
Manufactured in China. All rights reserved.
http://www.harperchildrens.com

Library of Congress Cataloging-in-Publication Data
Schlessinger, Laura.
  Why do you love me? / by Dr. Laura Schlessinger and Martha Lambert ; illustrated by Daniel
McFeeley.
      p.   cm.
  Summary: A young boy asks his mother why she loves him and learns that her love is unconditional.
  ISBN 0-06-027866-8
  [1. Love—Fiction.   2. Mothers and sons—Fiction.]   I. Lambert, Martha Lewis.   II. McFeeley, Daniel, ill.
PZ7.S347115Wh   1999   97-42203
[E]—dc21   CIP
                                                                                   AC

Why Do You Love Me?

By Dr. Laura Schlessinger

and Martha Lambert

Illustrated by Daniel McFeeley

Cliff Street Books

An Imprint of HarperCollinsPublishers

Sammy's mother finished his bedtime story and kissed him on the tip of his nose. This always made Sammy smile. "I love you," she said.

Sammy smiled again and looked at her.

"Why do you love me?" he asked.

This made Mother smile. "Why do you think I love you?" she asked.

Sammy thought for a moment.

"Because I'm so good at karate?" he asked.

"Or because I won the race last Saturday?" asked Sammy.

"Or because I picked up all my toys today?" asked Sammy.

"No," said Mother.

"You mean you don't care what I do?" asked Sammy.

"I care very much," said Mother. "I'm proud of you for trying your best, I love to see you having fun, and I appreciate it when you pick up your toys. But these are not the reasons I love you."

"Why not?" asked Sammy.

"Because you don't have to be good at karate, or first in a race, or always neat and tidy for me to love you," said Mother.

"Oh," said Sammy, still wondering why.

"Then do you love me because I helped Matthew when he fell down?"

"Or because I said you could use my bike to go to the store?" asked Sammy.

"Because I bring you juice in the morning?" asked Sammy.

"No," said Mother.

"Why not?" asked Sammy.

"When you are kind and thoughtful," said Mother, "it shows me the love in your heart, and that touches my heart, but that's not why I love you. I love you because you're the one and only Sammy there will ever be in the whole world—and you're mine. That's enough for me to love you all the time."

Sammy grew quiet. He thought for a moment or two and then asked, "Is there ever a time you don't love me?"

"No," she said.

Sammy looked surprised. "You mean you still loved me when I yelled at you yesterday?" Sammy asked.

"Or after I hit Peter for taking my truck?" asked Sammy.

"Or when I crayoned on the wall?" asked Sammy.

"Yes," said Mother, "I still loved you!"

"You mean you loved the things I *did*?" asked Sammy.

"No," said Mother, "I was very angry. I did not love the yelling, or the hitting, or cleaning off the crayon marks. But I still loved you."

"How come?" asked Sammy.

Mother grew quiet for a moment and then said, "Because, Sammy, the love in my heart is like the sun in the sky. It is always there, even when you can't see it."

"Like on a cloudy day?" asked Sammy.

"Yes," said Mother. "Exactly. When we are angry or sad, it is like a cloudy day and things seem very gloomy. But we know the sun is still there and—it will shine again."

Sammy thought for a moment. "But sometimes when I feel very angry with you, like when you send me to my room or say I can't play with Peter, I don't feel like I love you at all."

"I know what you mean, Sammy," said Mother. "It's hard to feel the soft feeling of love when you are feeling sad or angry or hurt."

"So what do I do?" asked Sammy.

"First of all," said Mother, "you are going to feel whatever you are feeling. Angry, sad, hurt, or lonely—whatever the feeling is—it's all right to feel it. But then take the time to remember that love is like the sun up in the sky. It is shining warm in your heart even on the angry, cloudy days."

"So that's how come you love me all the time . . .
no matter what?" asked Sammy.

"Yes," answered Mother. "No matter what."

"I'm glad," said Sammy, kissing his mother on the
tip of her nose.